I0819583

AND SIDE BY SIDE THEY WANDER

AND SIDE BY SIDE THEY WANDER

MOLLY TANZER

TOR PUBLISHING GROUP
NEW YORK

This is a work of fiction. All of the names, characters, organizations, places, and events portrayed in this work are either products of the author's imagination or used fictitiously.

AND SIDE BY SIDE THEY WANDER

A Tordotcom Book
Published by Tom Doherty Associates / Tor Publishing Group
120 Broadway
New York, NY 10271

www.torpublishinggroup.com

EU Representative: Macmillan Publishers Ireland Ltd, 1st Floor, The Liffey Trust Centre, 117–126 Sheriff Street Upper, Dublin 1, D01 YC43

The Library of Congress Cataloging-in-Publication Data is available upon request.

ISBN 978-1-250-38205-4 (hardcover)
ISBN 978-1-250-38206-1 (ebook)

First Edition: 2026

Printed in the United States of America

10 9 8 7 6 5 4 3 2 1

for John Kessel

But give them me, the mouth, the eyes, the brow!
Let them once more absorb me!

—Robert Browning, "Eurydice to Orpheus"

AND SIDE BY SIDE THEY WANDER

There were five of us on the spaceship, more or less: Tarquin Lennox, Tchik-tchik, Arakachi Misora, Jack Kirby, and me.

Our destination was the Greenwood, a museum on the other side of our galaxy. Earth's greatest works of art were currently on loan there, and had been for nearly three hundred years. We—humanity, I mean—had approved their removal. Unfortunately for us, the museum's founders and curators, the Celerians, were disinclined to give them back. All available evidence led to the conclusion that they'd never actually intended to do so—at least not on any timeline other than their own.

Our options were limited. A show of force from Earth was impossible, laughable. Not because Celerian technology was unbelievably more advanced than our own, though it was, but because ours was built on theirs, using their techniques, their code, their proprietary materials. They'd reminded us of this when we'd objected to their refusal to return what was ours. It would be no trouble for them to completely and permanently disable our whole planet from across the galaxy. They offered to prove it, if we wanted to pursue the matter.

We chose not to.

The Celerians accused us of ingratitude, which wasn't fair. We weren't ungrateful. Humanity's continued existence proved that. Back in the twenty-first century, the Celerians had helped us save ourselves from ourselves. In the scorching summer of 2037 they'd come in silver ships that looked exactly and nothing like we'd imagined in our science fictions. The same went for the people inside: like us, the Celerians were bipedal, minimally dimorphic, and warm blooded. Unlike us, they were covered in fine, lustrous gray fur and had prehensile tails, perfect for swinging through the trees they so loved.

They came in peace, they said, and with an offer: if we trusted them with the stewardship of Earth's art, they would provide us with the solutions to our multifarious but solvable problems. They were preservationists, they said. They wanted to protect humanity's legacy, for the benefit of the universe, and from our own recklessness.

Not all species are art-makers—at least not the visual arts, which the Celerians claimed was the rarest and most precious impulse of all. They had made it their mission to help those with the inclination. Art is a perishable thing, they said. We humans might marvel at our petroglyphs and pyramids, but in truth they have existed for only a moment of deep time. If we destroyed ourselves, even our more durable accomplishments would one day cease to exist. It would be as if they never were.

The Celerians could ensure their survival. They were a truly ancient species. They'd built their museum long before Earth's Cambrian Explosion, and in all that time it had never come to any harm.

The arrangement wouldn't last forever, not if we didn't want it to. At least, that's what they said. Once Earth was a safer place for our art—and our art-makers, those too, naturally—we could have it back. In the meantime, they would provide us with a universal vaccine, translation implants, an algae that fed on the plastics clogging our oceans, and the remarkable organic computers we called genesis trees. These biotechnological marvels were crucial to our species' recovery. Not only did they act as carbon scrubbers with their enhanced photosynthesis, they could be programmed to provide clean energy, and grow just about anything from personal communication devices to replacement bones and organs. They could even be used for sustainable housing.

The Celerians would also provide us with synthetic reproductions of the art they wanted to borrow, compositionally identical to the originals. Functionally the same, they claimed, and as many copies as we wanted. Every museum in the world could have its very own *The Birth of Venus*, every city its own Obelisk of Theodosius. So could every collector—at least, those with enough influence make their desire known to the right people.

It was a tempting offer. Along with all the other problems facing Earth at the time, sea level rise was threatening the museums of New York, London, Paris. Many of the more famous works of art had already been relocated. It was increasingly difficult to keep even small spaces climate controlled and free of ever more aggressive molds and microbes.

After some debate, Earth's leaders said yes.

The Celerians were delighted. They made their selections, gave us everything they promised, and disappeared, telling us to "get in touch" when we'd fixed things.

Well, we'd fixed things. It took a few centuries, but we got there. Mostly. By the Celerians' own standards, our climate-stabilized planet, where poverty was only a memory, was finally safe for our population and our paintings, our monuments, our pottery, and our sculptures. When we proudly told them this, via the ansible they'd gifted us, the response was not what we expected.

They said *no*. Actually what they said, before the conversation deteriorated into threats, was that they had no immediate plans to visit our part of the galaxy anytime soon. That's why a group of us decided if they wouldn't come to us, we'd to go to them.

My old friend Tarquin was our expedition's leader, but he wasn't the captain. That was Tchik-tchik, a designation that seemed to refer to both the individual we were working with, and their species as a whole. It was their ship. Humanity had managed some interstellar travel, but our vessels were not yet capable of journeys of such distance.

I admit I found Tchik-tchik terrifying. They were the first alien I'd met, ever. I'd never even heard of the Tchik-tchik before this voyage. My reaction might have been mere xenophobia, but also, they were well over two meters tall, with an insect-like appearance: many arms, segmented body, clacking mandibles. The Tchik-tchik are not insects, which to my mind makes the similarities worse.

Misora was our "muscle," as Tarquin put it, as if we were in an old heist movie. She was an ori-jin, a set of sextuplets folded into a single body using extremely illegal biotech, and an 8th dan in Goju-Ryu karate. I have no idea where Tarquin found her, but he had ever been an aristocrat and man of the world, and thus kept unusual company.

Amusingly, in manners and appearance, Misora was the least threatening person aboard. She was bubbly, tanned, and sported a bleach-blonde ponytail. She could, however, rip any of us apart, even when there was just one of her. I saw her working out a few times. She was pure muscle.

And then there was Jack.

Jack was a sensynth, a sentient synthetic being who could interface with computer systems with a supercomputer's speed and a human's intuition. Most importantly, Jack had been constructed way back in the twenty-first century. He was the most powerful machine intelligence on Earth without any Celerian augments, which meant there was no worry our alien adversaries could brick him if they caught us.

My name is Fennel Tycho, and my role was much less exciting. If you recognize my name, especially in conjunction with Jack's, you might guess what I was there to do. I was at one time Jack's attaché, his liaison, his handler—though that term is a fraught one, given the scandal that led to my dismissal. Perhaps I shouldn't assume you'll be familiar with the entire affair, to use yet another uncomfortable double entendre.

This is my chance to tell my side of the story. Finally; I was not allowed to give interviews at the time. Or now, technically. Ah, well. Even if I wasn't beyond the reach of the nondisclosure agreements I signed, I'm certainly past caring about them.

I realize I've begun in the middle of things. It's difficult to know where to start. I can't actually assume anything about who will find this recording, if anyone ever does. You might be a fellow human who already knows how we pawned our past for a shot at a future;

you may be a Celerian, smiling at my naïveté. Or you might be some unknown-to-me race of starfarers, millennia from now, when all that remains of me is this tale to be deciphered. There won't be any bones.

2

The Tchik-tchik vessel was all curves; no right angles or hard lines anywhere. The dark, subtly shimmering interior was made of a slick material that felt oily to my fingers. There were no adornments anywhere, no personal touches. What little furniture there was appeared to grow from the floor, though "floor" was a relative concept. Except in specific cases, the rooms and hallways had no *up* or *down*, not in the way I was accustomed to understanding those concepts. It was more like a big anthill in space. Tchik-tchik could climb and even hang upside down like a spider. We were issued gloves and booties that helped us cling to the walls, moving omnidirectionally when required. Even so, I never got used to the feeling of entering a gravitationally oriented room from the hallways. It always gave me a touch of nausea. I got turned around—literally—more than once.

I thought the vessel seemed small for traveling such long distances; then again, I had no frame of reference. We saw the cockpit, the mess, a common room, the cargo hold, the one bathroom that had been refitted for human needs, and our quarters—which Tchik-tchik explained were typically used for storage, not individual repose. "Tchik-tchik to fussing not, duty means to sleep around," they said, gesturing down the hallway. It was always interesting communicating with Tchik-tchik. Our translators didn't work so well with their clacking clicking language. I was just grateful our rooms had beds, even if they were clearly repurposed shelves. Tchik-tchik clung to a wall when they slept.

Once we were settled, Tarquin summoned us to the common room. There were a few data pads on the big central table, and he'd already set up a projector, screen, and a small holo-generator.

We stood. There were no chairs. The Tchik-tchik just fold their legs up under themselves to sit.

Tarquin was wearing a tweed suit cut perfectly for his lean body. His robin's-egg silk cravat accented the blue veins in his neck. "I expect you're all wondering why I gathered you here today," he said, his charming smile freshening up the moldy joke. "I know we've just arrived, and that our journey will take several weeks, but we've no time to lose."

"You sound like you're working up to telling us something bad," said Jack. He was slouching against the wall, looking cool as always in his black leather jacket and jeans. "If there's no time to lose, you'd best get on with it."

Tarquin looked annoyed to be interrupted, especially by Jack. They'd never liked one another. "Patience, my automatic associate," said Tarquin. Jack stiffened at this. Tarquin didn't give him a chance to object. "This is just a mission briefing. It's nothing bad."

I wasn't sure I believed him. In my experience, Tarquin always got very formal when he had to tell you something he knew you wouldn't like.

Tarquin turned on the little projector. On the screen appeared the image of a serene-looking bronze head in a crown, its face covered in markings. "The Ife Head," he said, and clicked through on his pad. "Van Gogh's *The Starry Night*, Banksy's *Love Is in the Bin*, Exekias' black-figure amphora depicting Achilles slaying Penthesilea, Kahlo's *The Two Fridas*, and the *Flying Horse of Gansu*." He turned back to us. "As you know, our mission is to swap out certain works of art being held at the museum with Celerian copies. These six are what I was able to acquire. They weren't easy or cheap to obtain, let me tell you." He grinned, and I felt my stomach tighten. Tarquin was definitely softening us up for a blow. "Ironic, isn't it? Their being so expensive, I mean. I suppose nowadays they're nearly three hundred years old so of course the price people ask for them is completely mad."

"Surely it's just a drop in the bucket for Lennox Enterprises," said Jack.

Tarquin got very quiet at this.

"Yeah, I thought we were going to bring back a bunch of stuff," said Misora, after too long of a pause. "I mean, I knew we weren't equipped to take back, like, Kinkaku-ji or the entire Terracotta Army. So why only these six?"

"Ah," said Tarquin, "yes. You see . . ."

His hesitation finally clued me in to what Tarquin didn't want to tell us. "Because Lennox Enterprises has nothing to do with this," I said. "We're on our own."

All eyes were on Tarquin now. For once he didn't like it, not one bit. "Look, this doesn't change anything," he said. "Not really."

"Tell us more about the 'not really' part," said Jack.

"Reduced cash flow has meant some compromises had to be made. Fewer works of art, and fewer resources than I'd hoped for. It's nothing to worry about! I have several pieces of original Celerian technology for you to explore, Jack. And while I couldn't find us a map of the museum, I did obtain an early blueprint."

"'An early blueprint'?" said Misora. "We are so fucked."

"We are *not* fucked!" said Tarquin, a little too loudly. "This is going to work," he continued, lowering his voice. "My shortsighted former colleagues and I may share a common genetic ancestor, but those clones have ever lacked our progenitor's vision. I believe in this venture—I mean, look at me, I'm here, I'm on the ship with you. I didn't just send you all out into the void with Tchik-tchik and hope for the best. I plan to succeed."

It was a good speech. I almost believed him.

3

Back in the twenty-first century, as part of their pitch, the Celerians had shown Earth's leaders their plans for the gallery that would display and honor humanity's material culture, the physical objects that made up our past. It was beautiful, like all Celerian engineering, a graceful upward spiral reminiscent of the old Guggenheim Museum, contained within a towering genesis tree, larger than any that grew on Earth. Individual branches would house our architectural marvels, whereas smaller works would be displayed in the trunk, prehistory down close to the roots, the then-modern age at the crown.

It sounded simple enough to navigate—or it might have been, if we'd had a map. Unfortunately, Tarquin's blueprint turned out to be even worse than I'd imagined. It wasn't even a complete file, just a screenshot.

I didn't have much to say as the team began discussing what they could do with what we had. This wasn't my purview.

I'd planned to get my Ph.D. in Art History and teach. Painting was my area, portraiture specifically. It was the lips. Thick or thin, pursed, pouting, or quirked, they were always where I found the deepest hints at meaning.

Some people say it's the eyes that draw one into a John Singer Sargent painting. I say it's the mouths—just look at Lady Agnew's. There is a secret, explicit and occluded, in her subtle smile. Caravaggio's Bacchus intrigues us with his expression. Vermeer's milkmaid is speaking something gently, perhaps reverently, into the quiet of an empty room. My thesis was tentatively titled "When Soul Meets Soul on Lovers' Lips: The Silent Language of the Mouth in European Portraiture, 1499–1999," and I had hoped to publish after I defended it.

Then my little brother died.

I couldn't believe it when they called me. Burnet couldn't be dead, he was the most *alive* person in the world. I was content in libraries. He climbed mountains, explored caverns, took submersibles to the bottom of the sea. He'd longed to go to space—a prospect that, ironically, had never appealed to me.

He'd been free-climbing the ruin of a skyscraper in what used to be New York City when he fell. His citizen tracker alerted the paramedics, but he was dead when they found him.

After his funeral I couldn't concentrate on anything—not researching, not writing, and definitely not grading. The endless cycle of the academic year felt depressing rather than comfortable; those painted mouths had nothing more to say to me. So I finished out the semester and went home, ostensibly to be with my parents as we grieved.

Rural Long Island is much as it has ever been, except without the appeal of being a train ride away from a thriving metropolis. I helped my mother in the garden and my father with the cooking. I made raspberry jam from the thicket growing around the trunk of our treehouse. Fine ways to spend a day, but I wasn't fine. I was going through the motions of a life without living one.

About six months after Burnet's death, just when I was really starting to spiral, Tarquin called me to offer his condolences. I agreed to meet him at a restaurant he'd taken me to many times back when we were both in school together in New Boston.

I said I'd take the solar train; he'd scoffed and sent a whirlybird. It had been an age since I'd been in one—probably since the last time I'd seen Tarquin. Our friendship had introduced me to the finer things in life such as private conveyances, which are widely disdained as an affectation of the wealthy. My father grumbled about what the neighbors would say. When I asked what neighbors he meant he switched to grumbling about the disturbance to my mother's garden.

As far as I could tell, nary a pea tendril was ruffled when the pilot touched down.

I dressed up for the meeting, or at least, I tried to. It had been months since my last haircut, or even since I'd really looked in the mirror. My face looked strange to me, touched up with mascara and blush, and the dress felt constrictive and weird. But I felt a little flicker of something when the black-clad pilot greeted me as "Miss Tycho" and opened the door for me, like my old self had taken a quick breath after holding it for so long.

The whirlybird touched down a few blocks from Quelque Chose, an exclusive but unpretentious French Revival restaurant. The interior was lovely: sparsely decorated and jungle-lush with plants, with huge windows that let in lots of light. Quelque Chose had always been too expensive for me—Earth was post-scarcity, but that never guaranteed gourmet dining for all. Tarquin, however, could afford the finer things, like the old-fashioned yet still stylish gray flannel suit he was wearing.

When I walked in, he was already seated and sipping a martini from a dewy glass. Always a gentleman, he stood and pulled out the bamboo chair for me.

"Would you like a cocktail?" he asked, as he signaled the waiter. I shrugged. He rolled his eyes and said, "She'll also have a martini—with extra olives, or she'll steal mine."

The silent waiter asked me with his eyes if this was right. I nodded.

Tarquin looked good; better than when I'd last seen him. He'd put on a bit of weight, and was merely pale, not wan. There were fewer lines around his pouty lips. He looked happy, and I said so.

"I *am* happy," he said, pleased—and then added, "and I'm as surprised as you are about that."

I took a sip of my cocktail. It was frosty and dry with just a snap of salt. I observed, but was unmoved by its perfection. "I didn't say I was surprised," I said.

"But you are. And that's entirely fair," said Tarquin, as some kind of pâté was set before us. I hadn't seen a menu. I assumed, correctly, that my companion had already done the ordering. "I got a job, Fennel! And I'm here to offer you one—or, well, to tell you to apply for one. You'll get it. I already told them about you."

This was typical Tarquin: magnanimous, scattered, elusory. Arrogant.

"Tell me about your job," I said, "and then tell me about the one you think I want."

"You'll want it," he said. "It's at Lennox Enterprises."

"That much I'd deduced, given the whole *happy* thing."

Lennox Enterprises is, or depending on when you're listening to this, was, the oldest and only corporation left on Earth. Founded by trillionaire Kirby Lennox in 2029, the company weathered the crises of the twenty-first century and the social upheavals of the twenty-second to thrive relatively unmolested in the stable twenty-third and twenty-fourth. It wasn't technically a corporation anymore—shareholder dividends and corporate law have been a thing of the past for a very long time—but Lennox Enterprises was allowed to operate much like they always had. The board of directors was entirely made up of Lennox's clones, as the original Kirby Lennox specified in his will, so there was a lot of legal uncertainty, and lack of precedent for a judicial dissolution.

Tarquin wasn't a clone. He was a Child of Lennox, and one with an impeccable pedigree. He was 100 percent Lennox stock, with genetics authenticated all the way back to Kirby Lennox's original pluripotent stem cells. Not all Children can make such a claim. Not all of them want to. Tarquin was exceptionally proud of his lineage, and had always possessed a massive chip on his shoulder regarding the clones, who tended to regard Children with suspicion, and vice versa. Securing himself a position at the company was a triumph, as well as a kind of vindication, given how he'd always viewed Lennox Enterprises with the entitlement and bitterness of an exiled prince.

"What's the job?" I asked as he preened. I hoped if I kept him talking he wouldn't notice I was just pushing my food around my plate. It was delicious, but none of it held any savor for me.

"I'm head of the effort to get the Celerians to talk about the return of our art."

This conversation took place about four years before I am recording this. At that time, the repatriation of Earth's material culture had been a deciding issue in the most recent global election. The candidate in favor of letting the matter go had won in a landslide. Public opinion had largely turned against the importance of "authenticity" when it came to art, but there were people who still cared about the fate of the real *The Night Watch*, original Rothkos, Sesshū's ink paintings, and so on, according to Tarquin. They'd turned to the private sector—specifically, to Lennox Enterprises.

Kirby Lennox was just as arrogant and sociopathic as a typical twenty-first-century trillionaire, but he'd fancied himself a philanthropist on the model of Rockefeller or Carnegie. Lennox built hospitals, funded schools, and was a dedicated patron of the arts. He spent much of his substantial fortune safeguarding works that had been passed over by the Celerians. In the centuries since his passing, Lennox Enterprises had continued this mission, at first by helping improve Earth enough that we could get back what we'd given away, and now by pressing on with the appeal that the Celerians had not received with generosity.

It was a big job, and a prestigious one. I raised my glass to toast my friend.

"Congratulations," I said, performing the enthusiasm I knew I should feel. "I assume the job you had in mind for me is related to this?"

He smirked. "Nope," he said, and signaled to the waiter that we'd like another round of drinks. "Saddle up, cowgirl. You're headed west, to the Great Mycelium. Turns out, it can talk."

When Earth accepted the deal offered by the Celerians, we did so as a planet.

It was the last thing the world agreed on for more than a century. The gifts intended for our salvation caused an inordinate amount of destruction because of *who* said yes. The legitimate, or perhaps I should say recognized, world governments of 2037 consented to the handover. There were plenty of other governments at that time. In North America, for example, the United States no longer had fifty stars on its flag. The area calling itself the New Confederacy, ruled from its capital city of Mar-a-Lago by a Large Language Model trained on speeches made by former president Donald Trump, was not a recognized country. Neither was an area in the Pacific Northwest called Cascadia. While that area was governed by actual humans, it had an even more radical agenda than the New Confederacy, driven by even weirder conspiracy theories, a willful misunderstanding of Christian scripture, and, naturally, racism.

In retrospect, it wasn't surprising they obtained a nuke. What was surprising was that they detonated it inside the Denver International Airport. The Cascadians believed that was where the Celerians had their "stronghold of influence," as they phrased it in their manifesto.

The distance from the former Denver International Airport to Denver proper meant many fewer lives were lost than there might have been. Unfortunately, the fallout drifted hundreds of kilometers into what was once Nebraska. The North Platte River was contaminated, and thus the Mississippi River would spread the effects. The United States needed to find a way to clean up the mess, and fast, even though public resources were scant.

Enter Kirby Lennox. Lennox wasn't just an art fancier. His company was mostly biotech. Before the Denver incident, the company had already bioengineered a radiotrophic fungus, based on specimens gathered from Chernobyl, to help in cleaning up nuclear disasters. The organism, which Lennox called *Cladiosporum lennoxspermum* to the annoyance of taxonomists, fed voraciously on radioactive contamination. The absorbed isotopes accumulated inside of truffle-like sacs that made for quicker collection and easier disposal in high integrity tanks.

C. lennoxspermum had proven its value during England's Hartlepool nuclear meltdown in 2033. Based on that success, Lennox made a convincing case to the United States government for using it in Colorado.

Lennox assured skeptics the fungus could never become invasive, that it would consume the nuclear contamination and die off once it had contained it. That did not end up being the case. Due to some last-minute tweaks to its genetics, the latest version of *C. lennoxspermum* inadvertently ended up able to feed not just on radioactive isotopes, but also the neutrons produced by the contamination. The voracious fungus surged north and west from ground zero, thriving on the extra cosmic radiation at altitude, spreading like a rust over grasses and trees and shrubs. The good news was it still contained the fallout as before, and as it grew it began to push these contaminated sacs to its edges. The bad news was that the mycelium had begun to replicate what it consumed, to duplicate what it absorbed. Within a month, the fungus had replaced all organic matter across the entire Front Range. Within a year, everywhere over 1600 kilometers above sea level had been subsumed. Entire communities had to flee their homes, and those that didn't . . . well, the video captured by drones was astonishing. Ambulatory fungal elk roamed across the high country, and things that looked like people lived in abandoned houses, doing strange imitations of people-things. Though it seems incredible now, at the time the fungus was just one problem among many, so humanity was forced to leave it alone.

After the world sorted itself out, humanity began to study the Great Mycelium—from a distance. Lennox Enterprises funded the effort, as reparations for their ancestors' role in the matter. There was another reason too, also tangled up with Kirby Lennox's ambitions: the Mt. Sanitas Art Preserve outside of Boulder, Colorado, the state of which was unknown after two hundred years of isolation.

Lennox had built five Art Preserves, placing them all over the world—or more specifically, in areas that gave Lennox Enterprises some kind of tax break. Secure, armored, with off-the-grid climate control, they'd been constructed to withstand anything imaginable. Unfortunately, no one had imagined the sinkhole that had swallowed nearly two million square kilometers of southern Siberia, destroying one of the preserves, or the Great Mycelium.

The Mt. Sanitas Collection was humanity's. Great works of art have always belonged to the world. Legally speaking, however, they were owned by Lennox Enterprises. Thus, my job would be spinning this effort to communicate with the Great Mycelium as altruism, making sure magazines and social media were full of compelling accounts of our discoveries, interviews with staff, the company's plans for the Art Preserve—if the efforts to access it proved successful—as well as making sure any editorials mentioning why the Mycelium existed in the first place, or questioning Lennox Enterprises' motives, were countered quickly and graciously.

At the time, I found the idea of being a corporate mouthpiece an amusing occupation for someone who had once spent a lot of time writing about lips. Now, I can't help but wonder if anyone will make a similar effort for our jaunt to the Greenwood. Tarquin certainly viewed our mission as heroic, for all humankind—even if no human had authorized our endeavor, and Earth's government would have sought to prevent us from going if they'd known about it.

Dinner that first night, which we ate standing, was a quiet affair. Tarquin's disclosures had unnerved us, and none of us were impressed that our leader had gone into business for himself. Tarquin, in turn, seemed annoyed. He'd expected us to take everything on faith; didn't understand why we weren't immediately convinced he had everything under control. But I'd known him for years, and I wasn't sure he believed it himself.

Eventually he admonished us to get some rest so we could get an early start the next morning, whatever morning meant on a starship, and departed for his quarters. After Tarquin left, Misora produced a deck of cards and proposed a game of Tycoon. I was curious to learn it, but Jack declined and headed to bed. This was no problem; Misora unfolded herself into two Misoras, so that we'd have the requisite three players. It was fun, once I got the hang of it.

Once she retired, I made my way back through the

bewildering corridors to Jack's quarters. He was already on his shelf, naked, one of his big hands tucked behind his head like a man relaxing on the beach.

He had a small Celerian tablet on his belly, clearly an original due to its irregular, organic shape. Human-made imitations tended to be cleaner, slicker, more squared off than the prototypes our benefactors had shared with us.

The interface was a screen, but also fluid—he'd sunk two of his fingers into the amber-colored gel, and a vine-like cable ran from the device into the pupil of his left eye. His right eye had rolled back in his head; it was completely white, and his eyelid was flickering.

I stood just inside the door, unsure if he knew I was there. After a moment his right eye reappeared to look at me.

"This thing is actually quite fascinating. I'd enjoy the experience of connecting with it if Tarquin wasn't expecting me to use it to learn how to hack a museum's security system."

"Do you think you can do it?"

"I don't know. His deception was foolish, and likely counterproductive. Little Lord Lennox should have been more up front about his intentions."

Due to a host of factors, from pollutants in food to unbalanced gut biomes, people of the twenty-first century had been a bit heavier, a bit taller, a bit thicker around the middle than modern humans—including Kirby Lennox. Made in his image, so was Jack.

I thought it was sexy. Like a god in a Rubens painting, he looked sensual, embodied, fleshy, even if he wasn't made of flesh. This voluptuousness had always drawn me to him, as did his affinity for casual nudity.

"I assume you came here for a reason," he said, sitting up on his sleeping bench. I could sense his amusement even if he wasn't smiling.

My cheeks flushed, and I nodded.

"That nod could mean anything. Speak."

He knew exactly why I was there, and he knew how hard it was for me to say it.

Jack set aside the data pad. "I don't have time for this," he said. "It will be faster if you just come over here and show me what it is you want. I need to get back to work."

I didn't particularly enjoy my PR job at Lennox Enterprises. To be fair, I wasn't enjoying anything back then. Burnet was never far from my mind. Little things reminded me of him—the scent of a food he'd liked, the idea of whitewater rafting when my boss suggested a team-building retreat. I still gave the job my best. I didn't want to embarrass Tarquin, who had stuck out his perfect, slender neck for me.

The skills valued inside academia are rarely useful outside it. Luckily for me, those hours spent researching and reading set me up to quickly comb through internal reports on communications attempts with the Mycelium, while monitoring news outlets and social media platforms to keep an eye on public opinion. Additionally, those papers and grant proposals I'd written helped me keep my press releases succinct, to the point, and for an audience. I did such a good job managing the public face of the Mycelium expedition that one of the clones from the board, K. Jasper Lennox, actually took a whirlybird to thank me personally, and handed me a bonus with hands unsettlingly similar to Tarquin's.

I did most of my work from behind my desk in Lennox Enterprises' Western Campus in Greeley, Colorado, the closest uncontaminated city to the Mycelium. There wasn't much there—never had been. That suited me. I liked the low humidity, it didn't snow as much as I'd thought it might, and my genesis treehouse had a view of the mountains. Best of all, no one knew me, so it was easy to keep to myself.

Around the time I arrived, there had been some exciting successes in furthering communication with the Mycelium. A few of my colleagues had volunteered to be partially colonized by spores, in order to facilitate even greater understanding between our species. I interviewed them a few times, collecting public statements for our press releases. It was fascinating—they spoke of comprehending the world on a deeper level, tasting new colors and textures, seeing new flavors. They'd had visions that they'd claimed had enhanced their understanding of the universe, and their place in it, and even the nature of life and death itself. It was difficult for them to put their experiences into words. Hearing them talk circles around it convinced me they'd been profoundly changed by the experience. Even so, I declined their entreaties to join them on the journey.

The volunteers negotiated limited safe passage through the Mycelium's borders, after assurances from

Lennox Enterprises and Earth's government of continued self-sovereignty for the Great Mycelium. This included leave to finally explore what remained of the Mt. Sanitas Art Preserve. Naturally, I was part of the effort.

They'd set up a decontamination zone in front of the ancient museum. After several tests to ensure we were free from any potentially destructive organisms, we finally cracked the door open. A puff of warm stale air hit us as if the building itself had sighed.

It was dark inside. The Mycelium had long ago coated the outside of the structure—the windows, the walls, the solar panels on the roof. It dampened sound, too. It was quiet in there, and our flashlights made the whole experience seem like an old horror movie, totally cliché—just like my shriek when I turned a corner and found you—I mean *him*, Jack, slumped insensate before a painting: Sir Frederic Leighton's *Orfeo ed Eurydice*. Actually, he was slumped in front of the electrical outlet beneath the painting; he'd rigged a way to donate his body's power to keep the environmental controls running as long as possible, to keep mold and other kinds of rot at bay.

Three days later, he woke up. I was there. I'd volunteered to keep an eye on him. I felt a sense of responsibility, given I'd been the one who'd found him, and I could do my work on my portable.

It was morning when he came to. I remember the day was fresh and crisp and alive with birdsong. Sunlight streamed in through the open window. I'd been working on a press release when I caught a flutter of motion at the edges of my vision and looked up to see him propped up on his elbows, staring at me with eyes that were hundreds of years old.

"Hello," I said. "How are you?" And then I blushed, realizing what a silly question that was.

"I'm not sure," he answered, taking me more seriously than I deserved. "I seem to have been rescued, so that's a good start."

I was charmed. Or maybe it would be more accurate to say I was fascinated, immediately and wholly. Whatever else Jack might have been, he was the first thing that had actually interested me since Burnet's death.

Was it so bad, what the Celerians did?

Wait—no. That's the wrong question.

Was it so *different* from what we humans have been doing to one another since we were humans?

We have always stolen: land, objects, people, culture, ideas. Human history is the history of theft. We loot, we raid, we imitate. We appropriate and misappropriate. The examples are too countless to name. Where could I begin a list? Where would I end it?

Yes, the Celerians took our art. One could, however, argue they gave us more than they removed—a claim that Rome had once made. England, too, and the former United States.

When I was in school I'd gone to museums whenever I could. Mostly I learned the history of art as students have always learned it: through reproductions—textbooks, digital images—all much less convincing than those made by the Celerians. It never bothered me; I'd never thought about it. Even when Earth's art was still on Earth, not everyone got a Grand Tour to see the Pont du Gard, the Colosseum, the naughty frescoes of Pompeii. For the vast majority of people the Venus de Milo might as well have been across the galaxy as in the Louvre.

Even so, I did feel differently when I looked at original works of art, and the reproductions always made me a little sad. I could never quite articulate why until I saw a real da Vinci. It was a minor one, hence why the Celerians had left it behind, but a minor da Vinci is still a da Vinci. The luminous, almost living quality of the work was wonderful, overwhelming, like a biblical angel whispering, *Be not afraid*. I marveled at the little signs here and there of the artist's brush, the care he'd taken layering the oils. The experience changed me the way only art can.

Later, when I saw my local museum's *Mona Lisa* for the zillionth time, I found it cold, repellent, unsettling. Many would say it was identical to the original in every way that mattered, but there was nothing there for me. What was meaningful was absent, like Burnet's lifeless corpse had been, when they called me in to identify his body.

Kirby Lennox had been of a similar mind. He agreed with Earth's choice—though to call it a choice implies we had any reasonable alternative—but felt compelled to ensure the safety of that which had been left. The

Celerians had taken away our greatest works. To him, that made the remaining ones all the more impossibly precious.

Thus, the Art Preserves. Lennox, beyond fond of his own image, had staffed them with sensynth curators fashioned in his likeness. He named them after his favorite artists: Lucian Freud, who had perished in the Siberian sinkhole; Hieronymus Bosch; Willem de Kooning (who has since changed her name to Elaine); Kitagawa Utamaro; and of course, Jack Kirby.

Lennox had rejected the so-called "artificial intelligence" products that caused so much trouble back in the early twenty-first century in favor of "synthetic sentience," a revolutionary new form of machine learning that produced genuine consciousness, complete with intuition, self-awareness, and emotions. His curators were among his finest creations. They were very different, individuals, more siblings than copies, with Jack being perhaps the most distinct of all.

I do not say that because I loved him. I say it because it is true. Jack's three surviving siblings were eager participants in the modern world—my world. They had updated themselves with Celerian technologies, augmenting their forms until they were hardly recognizable as copies of Lennox. They were political, mainly in the various campaigns for sensynth rights; celebrities with their causes célèbres.

Jack, on the other hand, was genuinely appalled by their behavior. He found their plant-cellulose enhancements from the genesis trees an aesthetic and philosophical self-betrayal. In Jack's opinion, they had been built to resist alien influence. How, then, could his siblings have surrendered their bodies to the same—and for the sake of style, or convenience?

While Jack enjoyed acting and dressing just like Lennox—who, like most of the twenty-first century's ultra-wealthy, had desired to be seen not as a CEO but a rockstar—his siblings had no interest in honoring the will of their long-dead creator. They found Jack's attitude offensive, especially because they had fought for their rights while he was still holed up in his museum. They told him in no uncertain terms that his old-fashioned attitudes had no place in the modern world.

On that point, and that point alone, Jack agreed with them completely.

If it seems odd that we had no strategy for helping Jack adapt to life in the twenty-fourth century, remember that we hadn't known whether or not he'd actually survived—and we hadn't thought it would be necessary. We'd assumed his sibling sensynths would step up, but he ticked them off so quickly and so completely that we had to improvise.

Jack may not have liked his siblings, but due to their efforts he was free to go anywhere he liked, do anything he wanted. Even so, the board of Lennox Enterprises asked him to stay with us on the Western Campus for a time. He agreed, and as Jack disliked me less than everyone else, I was assigned to be his attaché.

I was thrilled.

I realize I haven't made Jack's company sound appealing. It's true that he was aloof, often pompous, and occasionally casually cruel—a contrarian know-it-all who seemed to take great pleasure in making everyone around him feel wrong-footed. He was also smart, sometimes funny, and there was something about the way he always seemed dissatisfied that made me want to please him. When I made him smile, it felt like an accomplishment.

When I had the idea to record this story, *my* story, I thought if I could just explain how things were between Jack and me, it would make sense of everything that happened after—but I'm finding it's impossible to put into words. How can I possibly describe the tremendous amount of *feeling* he evoked in me, after I'd felt so much nothing, and for so long? When he touched me, my skin prickled to life; when he asked me if I'd like to go to bed with him, my pulse quickened. His laugh thrilled me when I asked, a little embarrassed, if that was even possible. His answer made my thighs clench together and my breath catch in my throat. *Do you think Lennox would create something that looked like him but couldn't fuck?*

I'll tell you about one conversation we had, one I ended up thinking about a lot after it was over—after *we* were over, I mean. We were in Jack's favorite place, the warehouse on campus where the Mt. Sanitas Collection was being kept for cleaning and restoration. I loved it, too. There was a minor Rodin, a Chagall, the original piece of duct tape that had once held one of the notorious "art bananas," a few uninspiring sketches by prolifics like Dalí and Picasso, and Judy Chicago's *The Dinner Party*—which, destined to be perpetually unappreciated for reasons I could never understand, had been left behind by the Celerians. This was especially insulting, to my mind, as they'd taken an original Thomas Kinkade, one with the little twinkle-lights.

Eventually we approached a piece I have already mentioned, Sir Frederic Leighton's *Orfeo ed Eurydice*, and paused before its radiant aura. The painting is an odd one. Orpheus resists Eurydice's embrace, pushing her away from him with gentle, if urgent, force. His eyes are screwed shut in determination as he rears his head back, exposing his white throat. His mouth is a thin line of resolve, while her lips are invitingly parted as she plucks insistently at the shoulder of his robe.

Orpheus's motive is clear. He is doing his best to obey the instructions of Hades. What strikes the viewer as curious is Eurydice's effort to tempt him even though she knows the consequence of failure. The strangeness of it had always tugged at me as insistently as Eurydice tugs at Orpheus's garment. I'd even written about it in my dissertation. It was a great painting for lips.

In most accounts of the myth, it is Orpheus who has the starring role. Ovid does not even include Eurydice among his *Heroines*. Leighton was a music lover, and his painted interpretation of the scene was very likely inspired by an opera by Gluck, whose librettist gave Eurydice a voice. Yet when she finally speaks, it is to tell Orpheus of her desperate need for a sign of his affection: his gaze.

This annoyed me back when I was working on my

thesis. Eurydice's insecurity exonerates her husband. It is no longer Orpheus's doubt that damns her, but her own.

Now I've changed. I disagree with my past self. Art can be a mirror through which we are shown ourselves—and who among us can claim to never have desired that which does not serve us? We are, at times, the agents of our own undoing, and in ways that likely seem obvious, even downright silly, to onlookers.

"Hold me but safe again within the bond of one immortal look!" I softly recited, quoting the verse Leighton's friend Robert Browning had written about the painting. *"All woe that was forgotten, and all terror that may be, defied,—no past is mine, no future: look at me!"*

Jack said nothing, gazing at the painting with such intensity I felt jealous. I thought again of Eurydice's final words—*look at me!*

Hoping he would, I said, "It reminds me of us a bit," then instantly regretted it.

Still, it made Jack turn to me at last. I was blushing horribly to have revealed myself so completely. He just looked confused.

"The story, I mean," I said, babbling out of insecurity, "not necessarily this painting of it."

"Why?"

It pained me that he didn't understand. I had no choice but to forge ahead. "Because I was dead when we met, or I might as well have been, and you brought me out of hell."

Jack considered this for a long moment while I, as anxious as Eurydice, plucked at his sleeve.

"Wasn't *I* the dead one?" he said at last, sounding amused, and not at all touched. "I mean, you rescued me, didn't you? You brought me out of the dark and back to life."

"Oh," I said. "I hadn't thought of that. I'm sorry."

"There's no reason to be sorry." His exasperated tone didn't make me feel any less foolish. "Either way, let's hope that's not the case. Orpheus fails."

9

After a few days aboard the Tchik-tchik vessel we'd adjusted to the ship's layout and time, and established our various routines. The mood had lifted a bit—planning was going fairly well, especially given what we had to work with.

This burgeoning sense of camaraderie did not extend to Tarquin. Jack loathed the man, and Misora would not forgive him for misleading us.

At first, he tried to ignore it. Tarquin kept cracking jokes and carrying on as if nothing were amiss. As the journey continued, however, he became increasingly frazzled. He began to avoid mealtimes, and abandoned the little gentlemanly flourishes that were his stock-in-trade. He left Misora to go through the schematics on her own and spent more time with Tchik-tchik in the cockpit. What he was doing in there was a mystery. When, in a misguided attempt to be sociable, I asked him what he was up to, he snapped at me to mind my own business.

But what *was* my business? I had completed the most important part of my contribution to the mission—finding Jack and convincing him to sign on—before our team convened in New Boston. Now that we were under way, my duties, according to Tarquin, were to ensure Jack's continued compliance by "keeping him happy." Whether I'd ever been able to do that was something I'd asked myself more than once, and without ever being able to decide on an answer.

Back when I was in college, I had a friend who declared, in the most matter-of-fact way imaginable, *"Love without reciprocation is obsession."*

I don't remember the context, or if there was one beyond our being students who were drinking. I do remember finding it incredibly provocative. This surprised him, and we had, if not an argument, an intense conversation about it; a little drunken Symposium of our own.

He thought his view was self-evident. How could unrequited love be anything other than an idée fixe? A person pining away for someone who never thinks about them is in the throes of fixation, not passion.

I declared the entire idea absurd. How could someone else's sensations define our own? What, I asked, about our feelings for the departed? And what of the unfortunate who is being deceived? Is someone who believes a lying lover also guilty of obsession?

What about a stalker, he asked. A stalker is not in love with the object of his desire.

People do all sorts of things while in love, I replied. Cheat, leave, yell—even kill.

That's not love, he said.

I shrugged. Are you sure? I replied. It seems to me that when people say, *That's not love*, while talking about behavior like stalking, what they actually mean is *I would never do that*. Or more accurately, *I hope I never would*.

I loved you, Jack. I know I did. I know I do. What I don't know is if you—he, I mean, *he*—loved me back.

When I asked, he warned me he wasn't sure he could. Jack said he experienced desire, craved sensation, enjoyed company. When we were together, I felt no detectable difference compared to other relationships of mine, other loves. At the time, I was certain that meant he loved me. Now, I'm not so sure. Maybe my friend was right. After it was over, after Jack left me, what was it that I continued to feel for him? Was it love? Or was it something else that made me pause and listen in, when I overheard him talking to Misora in the common area?

This is what they said:

Jack said, "I can't stop looking at it."

"It's amazing," replied Misora. "I went to the planetarium as a kid, but nothing could've prepared me for *this*."

We'd docked at a Tchik-tchik "hub-hive" to refuel. Only Tchik-tchik had left the ship—*For you intact bodies to stay safety*, they said, before forbidding even Tarquin to come along. The hub looked much like a cosmic hornet's nest, viscerally repulsive. Jack and Misora were gazing out past it and into the deep blackness of outer space where the stars were unfamiliar, bright, and glorious. When the Tchik-tchik ship was in motion there was nothing much to be seen, so this had been our first opportunity to get a look at space from space.

"No facsimile can ever prepare anyone," said Jack. "The attempt to mechanically reproduce something numinous only ever serves to diminish it."

I clung to the smooth, slick, almost oily-feeling wall, not moving, barely breathing. I knew it was wrong to eavesdrop, but I was enjoying the sound of Jack's voice, imagining the familiar shape of his lips as he spoke.

"Do you really believe that?" asked Misora.

"I have no doubt whatsoever. And neither do our Celerian friends. Think about it—they may claim their reproductions are no different from our originals. If that was the case, why wouldn't they have taken their reproductions and left us our art?"

Misora considered this. "What about *The Starry Night* in the cargo bay?"

"What about it?"

"Obviously that one's a copy. So how is van Gogh's painting—the original one, I mean—how is it different than the planetarium? Isn't his painting of the sky . . . diminishing the numinous?"

"No! No, absolutely not!" Of course that was what

Jack said; there was no other answer he could give and still be himself. "A work of art is a unique expression of radical subjectivity, made by a person, in a place, in a time, with an intention."

"A photograph isn't?"

I'm not sure why I did what I did next. No, that's not true. I know *exactly* why I swung into the common area, as if I'd just been passing by and happened to overhear them. I wanted to show off—or maybe just show Jack that I agreed with him.

"Intention makes all the difference," I said. "A planetarium doesn't have the same goal as, say, Ansel Adams. But even Adams's photographs have a degree of loss. They're beautiful, but they're not the same as being at Yosemite when the snow is blowing and the moon is out."

I was hoping—longing—for a look of approval from Jack. He was too eager to continue on with his point.

"Yes, *yes*," he said. I had to be content with that; pathetically, I was. "Think about being back on Earth and looking up at the moon on a clear evening. There's something about that experience that has inspired artists throughout human history. And through what the philosopher Walter Benjamin called 'a strange weave of space and time' you experience something intimate, even though the moon is far away. That's because the distance between you and what you're looking at is *real* in that moment. No photograph could possibly capture that experience."

"That's true," said Misora. "Every time I've taken a picture of the moon it's always terrible. I've never understood why."

"Photography can't capture the experience of subject and object existing in the same moment in time and space. Mechanical reproductions artificially reduce distance. Think about it this way: what feels closer to your experience of gazing out at the universe—your trip to the planetarium or *The Starry Night*?"

In that moment I thought back to a starry night, when Jack and I had had a similar conversation on the banks of the St. Vrain River, just on the border of the Mycelium. We lay on our backs in the damp grass, looking up at the moon and the stars through the spreading branches of the cottonwoods. *Have you ever seen anything so beautiful?* I'd asked, as fireflies blinked above us. He'd turned to look at me, and I saw everything reflected in his eyes except myself. *Rarely,* he'd said, *and I spent two centuries with little to look at but works by the masters.* As usual, I couldn't tell if he was being romantic or simply descriptive. I kissed him anyway, and he kissed me back, and I was, in that moment, content.

Misora brought me back to the present. "Probably the painting," she said.

"Exactly." Jack was not lost in thought—or if he was, his synthetic brain was able to reflect on both things at once. "That's because *The Starry Night* isn't a painting of a starry night. It's a painting of van Gogh's experience of a starry night. He wasn't trying to reproduce reality; he was gifting us his unique version of it."

We fell silent to gaze a bit longer upon the fathomless cosmos, peaceful and contented, until Misora asked a final question—the worst question she could possibly ask.

"So, do you think you could tell?"

"Tell what?"

"It's pretty easy to tell the planetarium from the universe," she said. "If we played a shell game with the faux van Gogh we have on board and the original—if we mixed them up and put them side by side—do you think you'd know which was which?"

I winced, and from the snarling twist of Jack's lips, I'd guessed correctly how angry this would make him.

"No," he snapped. "And that's the worst part—but I can't expect *you* to understand."

And with that he brushed past me and into the corridor beyond, leaving Misora looking confused and a bit annoyed, and leaving me with a rising sense of panic. I pushed a thought aside for later.

"I was only asking," she said crossly.

"It's a fair question," I said. My voice sounded faint in my ears.

"*He* can't expect *me* to understand?" Misora sucked her teeth. "I understand pretty well, I think! Maybe not about art, but I mean . . . there are six of me folded inside me. After we split and come back together, I'm never sure which one I am. I mean, how would I know if I was different? I'd think I was the same, wouldn't I?"

"I don't know," I said.

"No, you don't. And neither would he—there's only one of him. So what the hell's his problem?"

I knew exactly what Jack's problem was.

The Celerian reproductions unnerved me. Jack *hated* them—and he hated the Celerians for making them. To him, the replacements were grotesque mockeries. He was not impressed by their uncanny precision; he was insulted by it.

I understood the anxiety at the heart of Jack's discomfort. He was a sensynth, an artificial being. He had the body of a human, wore the face of a human—the most recognizable human face in the world. But he was not the reproduction of a human—of Kirby Lennox—any more than Tarquin was, or Lennox's clones. There were times when I wondered if *he* saw himself that way, or at least worried about it.

Not only that, but Jack's body, his mind, the whole of his being—he was, hypothetically, reproducible. If a Celerian van Gogh was truly indiscernible from a real one, what would it mean if someone made a copy of *him*?

That night he didn't come to me, nor did I go to him. I didn't want company. I had too much on my mind. I was musing on our conversation in the common room; specifically, Jack's reaction to the question of whether anyone could actually tell an original from a fake.

That's the worst part.

He was right about that.

I think back to my experience with the da Vincis, real and imitation. At the time, I'd been so certain of the difference. I'd felt it, the liveliness of the original and the absence in the duplicate. Then again, the museums had told me which was which. I had no such exegesis to consult regarding my relationship with Jack. Our affair had felt more passionate, more real to me than any other. I know that may have been a referendum on the insignificance of my past intrigues, not a reflection of his feelings, if he truly ever had them. In the absence of an authority to tell me what was real and what was fake, it's possible I was bamboozled by a forgery.

12

Misora had mapped out the Earth Gallery and come up with several plans for how we could swap out our various fakes. In order to facilitate discussion she'd enlarged the holo-schematics with Jack's help, and added various glowing lines that snaked through the trunk to show potential paths. Unfortunately, there was no perfect solution to our problems, and deciding on the best route proved contentious.

"I still vote for starting at the top and heading down," said Misora. "It'll be faster—and it'll mean we can unload the unwieldy paintings first."

"There's no unobtrusive place to dock," said Tarquin. He'd made this point several times already, and seemed exasperated. "The best place for that is here." Tarquin pointed to one of the lower branches off the main trunk, a large one earmarked for housing ancient architectural marvels. "There's an emergency access panel and air lock."

"And there's an elevator nearby," I said. "We could dock at the bottom, then take the lifts to the top of the tree and work our way down."

"If my calculations are correct, the Exekias amphora will probably be below that air lock," said Jack. "If we had more up-to-date plans, we might know for sure . . ."

"It's one item," said Misora, when Tarquin's face turned red. Jack and Tarquin had already gotten into several bickering matches, and Misora and I were tired of their squabbling. "If you wanted, we could even go down to do that one first, then head to the top."

"The vase is the most fragile," I said. "Do we want to carry it around the longest?"

"What if we dropped it off on the way?" said Tarquin.

"That'll take longer," said Misora.

"Not if I do it," I said. "I could head down there while the rest of you head up, drop it back at the ship, and then join you up at the top."

"Alone?" said Misora.

"Why not? The elevator's right there. It'll be easy."

"With all six Misoras, there will be enough of us that you won't even need to join us," said Jack. "You could just hang back with Tchik-tchik."

"Oh!" I said. I didn't like the idea, but it seemed frivolous to argue that, independent of our mission, I'd like to see the museum.

"Should we even be using the elevators?" said Misora. "Won't that tip off their security systems?"

"You brought me along to disable those kinds of

alerts," said Jack. "I should be able to access those systems through the emergency panel."

"What about before that?" I asked. "Won't they see us coming?"

"Don't worry," said Tarquin.

"Why not?" asked Misora.

"Tchik-tchik's handling it," he said. "That's what they're here for. We need to focus on getting inside, and what happens after."

Before we could discuss this further there was a crackle, and Tchik-tchik's clacking voice came in over the ship's communication system.

"It is to arriving," they said. "Possible see museum wishing you now?"

13

Tchik-tchik had brought us down on an asteroid close to the museum, the ship clinging like a tick to its far side. We gathered in their small cockpit to get our first look.

All we could see was a forest of branches spreading into space. Later, when I saw the whole structure, I understood. The Earth Gallery was only one of many. The entire museum was like a forest world, innumerable, enormous genesis trees radiating outward from a central circular root ball. It was a sobering sight. The Celerians told our ancestors that art preservation was their mission, but it hadn't ever occurred to me just how many species might need their art kept safe off-world. I wondered what sad situations had caused these other beings to surrender their material culture. Had they, too, mismanaged themselves into catastrophe? Or had their worlds been threatened by disasters of a different sort?

"So they don't know we're here?" asked Misora.

"No being worry," said Tchik-tchik. "Ship is bamboozle fancy tree. Pheromone emit, is shield. Not see now, not know when ship land."

This struck me as strange. Before I could ask any questions, Tarquin spoke up.

"When can we go in?" he asked.

Tchik-tchik shrugged lackadaisically. "Is to desire we going."

"So anytime," said Tarquin.

"Regardless, the sooner the better, I'd say," said Jack.

"Well, yes, *naturally*," said Tarquin, once again annoyed with Jack. "I guess then the question is . . . are we ready?"

"I'm not sure more arguing will be helpful," said Jack. "I think the general idea of Fennel taking care of the amphora while the rest of us head up and then down again makes decent sense. We'll know more after I hack into their systems."

"Fine," said Tarquin. "Get yourselves together and meet me in Cargo Bay Two in an hour."

Jack and Misora left. I stayed behind. I had a question for Tarquin.

"Got a minute?" I said, as he wrangled himself out into the hall.

"Sure," he said. I heard caution in his voice. "What can I do for you?"

"I guess I was just wondering about Tchik-tchik . . ."

"What about them?"

"It seems a bit strange to me that their ship just happens to be able to hide from Celerian defenses."

"Oh." Tarquin paused, as if considering what to say. "Well, they use pheromones—or something—for everything. The intercom is for us. Under normal circumstances they use the ventilation system to communicate."

"If they're on friendly terms with the Celerians . . ."

"Who said they were?"

That took me by surprise. "What?"

"It's none of our business whether they are or not. Our quarrel is with the Celerians—"

"Is it a quarrel?"

"They have our art. We've earned the right to get it back, by their own benchmarks. They said no. If the Celerians didn't want us to explore other solutions, they should have worked with us in the first place. So now the Tchik-tchik are helping us, and at no real cost to us."

"What do you mean 'at no real cost to us'?"

I could tell Tarquin was getting annoyed from the supercilious way he was looking down his aristocratic nose at me. "They wanted the coordinates of the museum, which I had. What they plan to do with them is no concern of mine."

I stared at Tarquin in horror. Back when he'd first recruited me—back when I believed this was a venture approved by and funded through Lennox Enterprises—it had never occurred to me to ask these kinds of questions. Now it was too late, and the answers were all terrible. I'd always known Tarquin had the kind of devil-may-care attitude to life that so often comes with wealth and privilege, but this was beyond reckless.

"It seems like it should be a concern. What if they mean the Celerians harm?" I asked. "What if they're evil?"

Tarquin scoffed at me. "That's very small-minded of you, assuming the bug-eyed monsters are bad. They're not *evil,* Fennel. Tchik-tchik rescued me. I met them when I'd taken one of our Earth ships and tried to get to the museum on my own. It was too far. I broke down. It was an amazing bit of luck that Tchik-tchik found me."

"Sure. What else do you know about them?"

"Beyond their generosity toward stranded space-farers? Not much. I'm the only person on Earth who's met them—who even knows about them! All of the Tchik-tchik, I mean, not just our Tchik-tchik."

This was news to me—alarming news. "Tarquin, I think—"

"Then stop." Tarquin smiled at me. It wasn't a nice smile. "You're not here to think, Fennel. You're here to keep the metal man under control so I don't throw him out the air lock before he has a chance to be useful. Understood?"

14

This is what happened between me and Jack:

About a year after Jack's rescue, things had grown strained between us. He was unhappy. Jack hated being in the public eye, but the clones wanted him there, to bolster their company's image. There had been some troubles with the whole Mycelium endeavor; several of the colonized volunteers had sickened after the Mycelium alleged there had been some unapproved removals of its substance. Lennox Enterprises needed some successes in the news, and Jack was a success. Sort of. At least he had been rescued, revived. He was a human-interest story even if he wasn't technically human.

Jack thought the bigger story was the restoration of the Mt. Sanitas Collection. The clones disagreed. Privately, I was on Jack's side—but Lennox Enterprises was my employer, and I was having trouble pleasing both. My managers knew I could only push him so far, but they clearly felt I could push a bit harder. They didn't know we were having an affair; didn't understand that with every confrontation I was risking something that mattered even more to me than my job. And Jack didn't appreciate my position at all—in fact, when I dared mention it, he became even more irascible and ungrateful.

It was a mess.

It came to a head about a week after a particularly embarrassing moment for the company. An intrepid journalist discovered that parts of the Mycelium had indeed gone missing, and those bits had ended up in the hands of one of Lennox Enterprises' subsidiary companies—one known to still dabble in weapons technology. The next day, two of the colonized volunteers died, and the initial autopsy reports could not rule out fungal aggression.

Lennox Enterprises needed a distraction. They decided on the "Ex Machina" benefit dinner, a glitzy, celebrity-studded event in New Boston seeking to raise awareness for the effort to place a total ban on human use of machine intelligence, a cause spearheaded by none other than Jack's most radical sibling: Hieronymus Bosch.

Hieronymus believed that *any* use by humans of machine intelligence was unethical, even the limited ones companies like Lennox Enterprises used to manage everything from temperature regulation of their buildings to malware neutralization. The cause had become very popular with the public after several such programs were shown to have become self-aware, and gone unnoticed—or possibly ignored—by companies and governments.

Jack considered this debate silly and annoying. In his opinion, the emergent intelligences in question were rudimentary at best, and he found the idea that he had anything in common with them insulting. He did not consider himself a machine intelligence, but a synthetic sentient being. Even so, after Lennox Enterprises sent a clone to talk to him, he agreed to make a rare public appearance.

The evening was a disaster.

Jack's brother Hieronymus was a forceful personality. He was the leader of the sensynth separatist movement and had so extensively modified himself that he no longer looked human. Taking inspiration from his namesake, he sported a birdlike beak for a face, many extra eyes of all sorts, and his body was covered in patches of fur, scales, and skins of textures and colors not usually found on humans. He had a prehensile tail crowned with spikes and two extra arms—one birdlike, one robotic in an old-fashioned sort of way.

His speech that night was deliberately incendiary. Speaking to an audience of humans and sensynths, Hieronymus did not stop at calling for an end to the use of machine intelligence in businesses and the medical industry. He claimed such tools philosophically de-personed sensynths. He spoke of the need for a sensynth-only colony apart from humankind—and, alarmingly to me, a voluntary end to all human-sensynth relationships.

Jack was visibly unimpressed. At one point he leaned over to me and whispered, loudly, "Can you believe this horseshit?" That earned him some dirty looks and whispered complaints. The real fireworks began when Hieronymus listed the ways that sensynths had surpassed humanity.

"Just look at me," said Hieronymus, gesturing at his body. "While humans fretted over the loss of their material history, I was busy remaking myself into a greater work of art than they ever produced. Behold! What use is mimesis when beings such as myself have embraced constant change? What use is abstraction when subjects like me can resist attempts at representation? What human work of art can be considered more important than what I have achieved?"

"'Achieved'?" said Jack, loudly enough that everyone around him could hear—as well as Hieronymus, with his superior senses.

"Brother, you wound me," said Hieronymus, as everyone in the banquet hall looked on. "I had hoped your appearance here tonight meant you had finally begun to see the truth—or are you still so fettered to your origin that you purposely deny your own potential?"

"Do you use that tail to balance? What do you need

those extra arms for?" Jack shrugged. "You're pretty, brother—but are you art?"

Hieronymus began to shout, and he wasn't the only one. The uproar was incredible. Not liking the situation one bit, and knowing the clones at Lennox Enterprises would like it less, I got Jack away from the reporters and paparazzi who were only too happy to record everything, and into one of the event center's greenrooms.

"I shouldn't have asked you to do this. I know you hate it," I said, after closing the door. "I'm so sorry. This is my fault, I know I've pushed you . . ."

Jack stopped pacing and looked at me with those uncanny eyes of his. His lips relaxed from a tense line into a small smile.

"I didn't do this because of you," he said. "I've been petitioning the board to keep the Mt. Sanitas Collection together, under my management. I agreed to do this to curry some favor, though I'm not sure I did my cause any good out there. I just couldn't take it! The arrogance of Hieronymus . . ."

We were alone in the room. We thought we were safe. He took me in his arms and he kissed me, and it felt like our first kiss all over again: sweet and entirely unencumbered by the burden of acquaintance. Alas, I'd closed the door without locking it, and Hieronymus chose that moment to barge in on us. We sprang apart like two teenagers too late; he'd seen us.

"I should have known," he sneered. "No wonder you

won't join with your sensynth siblings, Jack. You're into *meatballs*."

"Get the hell out," said Jack.

"We're not yours to toy with as you please!" said Hieronymus, now speaking to me.

"I'm not toying with him!" I protested. "I love him!"

"This is none of your business," said Jack, and pushed his sibling out of the room. I couldn't help but notice he never said he loved me back.

We left separately that night, both uneasy. We had reason to be. The next day, we were called in for an ominously early meeting. Several Lennoxes were there; they must have flown in overnight. Even though they looked alike, each looked unhappy in their own way.

The news of our relationship had already hit social media. They asked us to explain. All we could do was apologize. I told them the truth, that concealing the affair had seemed like the best course, given my position at the company. Jack agreed. He'd wanted me to remain his attaché after the relationship began, but hadn't thought they would allow it.

"You're right about that," said K. Barnaby Lennox.

"You've embarrassed the company," said K. Everett Lennox. "Miss Tycho, I'm afraid we have no choice but to let you go."

"What about the Mt. Sanitas Collection?" asked Jack. My stomach tightened up when I realized that its fate was his priority in that moment, not mine.

"There is no Mt. Sanitas Collection," said K. Barnaby. "Not anymore. We intend to sell it off to various museums."

"*Why?*" Jack's voice cracked on the question. I had never witnessed such a display of emotion from him as in that moment.

"For one thing, it's yet another reminder of this entire disastrous endeavor with the Mycelium—"

"That collection endured hundreds of years of isolation and neglect. It can survive a news cycle!"

K. Barnaby shook his head impatiently. "It's not just that, Jack. The collection is no longer an asset to this company. The public simply doesn't care about it—and why should they? It's been centuries! Humanity has continued to make art, and we have the reproductions, which are identical in every important way."

"If that's true, why don't you walk straight into the Mycelium right now, and let whatever walks back out again serve on your precious board?"

The clones had nothing to say to that. Neither did they look convinced.

"I see," said Jack. "Well then . . . if you're liquidating the collection, I have no reason to stay."

And with that, he got up to leave. As I watched him walk out on us, the Browning verse came to me again: *No past is mine, no future: look at me!*

He did.

He looked back; his eyes met mine. "Jack," I said, reaching out to him. He turned away and slammed the door behind him, leaving me behind to slip

slip

slip

back

down

into

hell.

15

Jack was long gone by the time I got out of that awful meeting. He'd just walked out through the front door. No one could stop him. Jack was a free being, so Lennox Enterprises had to concoct a crime to justify the ensuing manhunt. They claimed Jack's synthetic brain had been programmed to record everything, and that meant he was in possession of classified material. Their efforts were to no avail. Unencumbered by modern technology as he was, there was no way for the modern world to track him. He simply disappeared.

Two years later, Tarquin contacted me about his new effort to get Earth's art back from the Celerians. I figured why not. I wasn't doing anything important, floating from hobby to hobby, from job to job, so I signed on to the project.

I thought at first Tarquin wanted me for my expertise in art, but no. He'd figured if anyone knew where Jack had gone, it would be me.

I hadn't known, but I'd long harbored a suspicion. It turned out to be correct. It was where I would have gone to get away if it hadn't been for two things, the citizen tracker embedded in my wrist, and the fact that I was organic: a faraway place on the banks of the St. Vrain River, on the ill-defined border of the Mycelium, the threat of which a sensynth like Jack need not fear. There among the cottonwoods he'd built himself a shelter out of sight of any whirlybirds, and there he welcomed me with open arms, as if you—I mean he—had been expecting me.

16

Our approach went just as Tchik-tchik promised: smooth and seemingly unnoticed. We gathered in the cargo hold, among the crates of Celerian fakes and other gear while they maneuvered the ship into position. Getting in and out of there was one of the wooziest maneuvers on the ship—that's how we'd boarded, so it had been a crash course in the varying gravities of the vessel. The ship had been engineered to dock perpendicularly, so the room ran up through the center of the vessel. There was a floor, on the stern side, and its exterior door was on the ship's belly—but it did not face "down." It faced outward, which was sometimes the same thing, though not always.

The emergency panel and entrance were on the side of a branch. I felt us alight and suction onto it.

"Are we ready?" asked Tarquin, once Jack ambled in, last as usual.

"I am," said Misora. She'd donned a skin-tight jumpsuit so black it absorbed light. It messed with my senses if I looked at it for too long; it made her body look perfectly flat, like a paper cutout. The effect was especially unsettling with the gun belt slung low on her slender hips, cowboy style.

She was the only one dressed for a fight; Jack hadn't changed, and Tarquin was in a natty suit as usual. I wasn't wearing anything special. "Light layers," some stretchier pants, shoes I knew I could run in.

"I'm ready, too," said Jack.

"Let's open her up, then," said Tarquin.

"Delighting," said Tchik-tchik.

The cargo hold door was like the aperture on an old camera, or maybe an orifice—it could tighten and widen, dilating as necessary. Some kind of transparent purple force field stopped us and everything else from being blown into space. It was also movable; Tchik-tchik could position it wherever they liked. They joined us after docking and proceeded to fiddle with some strange instruments; eventually, they used their mantis-like forelegs to open the ship up on top of an amber-colored panel that looked like it had grown out of the surrounding bark, like a canker or burl. Tchik-tchik made a few adjustments and the crackling field lowered enough that the panel was technically inside the ship.

Jack poked his fingers into the gel. After a moment, there was a big jolt and some rusty aftershocks. Tchik-tchik went back to the cockpit and spoke orders to Tarquin through the comm, as they readjusted the ship's position.

The ship's aperture closed, then opened wider and wider until it revealed a doorway that appeared when one strip of bark slid behind another. The tunnel beyond was large enough for Tarquin to walk through it without stooping, and there was some kind of chamber on the other side, just like the museum plans had shown.

There was another amber-screened computer terminal inside the tunnel. Once the ships were aligned, Jack jumped through and immediately set to work. His focus was absolute—he went completely still after hooking up his eye and sinking his whole hand into the screen. Everything went just like his trial runs with the antiques, and I felt better about our mission than I had since our first day on the ship, until Jack started spasming like he was having a fit.

He collapsed to his knees, hand still stuck in the goo. Without a thought in my head beyond Jack's welfare I ran to his side, into the museum, and put my hand on his shoulder. I had the terrible thought that maybe Tarquin had been wrong, and the Celerian tech could brick my lover. "Jack," I said into his ear. "Jack, come back, please."

After a breathless moment or two longer, Jack stirred. His unattached eye focused on me.

"I'm all right," he said, as I helped him up. He began disconnecting himself. "I just got a little lost in there. It's more sophisticated than those antiques Tarquin had me working with—but not by as much as I thought. Anyway, I disabled their alarms systems, including the pressure panels on the floors and some kind of ambient carbon detector that would have registered your exhalations. I downloaded an actual map into my mind, too."

"Where are we?" Tarquin had joined us. "What's inside?"

"The Parthenon. Our estimations were surprisingly good."

"Excellent," said Tarquin. "Let's get to it."

I looked back at the cargo bay as Misora shuddered and split into six, like an accordion expanding and then breaking apart. Only one had the gun belt, and I thought back to our conversation in the observation lounge. Which one of her carried the weapon? Did it matter? Not at the moment at least—they were very much in tune with one another as they began to open the crates with the Celerian fakes, distributing them among themselves, two Misoras for *The Two Frida*s, as it was a large canvas. Tarquin hovered, but did not direct them, which was smart of him. I noted how no one objected to *him* going along with the bigger group, even though he served no meaningful purpose. I didn't comment on that—not even when he said, "Careful with that," to me, as I picked up the amphora.

"Thanks for the advice," I said.

"Our hive the universe it exists," said Tchik-tchik, waving at us with one of their arms. Tarquin said it meant *good luck*.

Jack led us through the tunnel and out into the bright ambient light of the chamber beyond. The walls were the soft color of untreated pine, and little leafy branches sprouted here and there. It really was like being inside a tree trunk, one larger than a cathedral—large enough to contain the Parthenon.

I've never been religious. My father was Jewish by birth but not by practice, and my mother was a lapsed Episcopalian, which made me nothing. I'd grown up devoid of reverence. My only experience of the transcendent has ever been through art. I felt it in that moment, before the silent, ancient monument. I felt its power radiating from the stone as we walked through the temple, and it occurred to me that its various friezes and pediments had never made it back to Athens before being whisked away to the other side of the galaxy. This fact was noted on the tombstone on the wall, close to the archway to the main gallery. It was a curious detail to include along with a quick history that mentioned the Delian League; the Parthenon's various reincarnations as a church, gunpowder magazine, and tourist attraction; and the chemical composition of the Pentelic marble used in its construction. It frustrated and saddened me to see the history of such an amazing structure reduced to data points, a list of facts like a child might look up in an encyclopedia. Museum descriptions are as political as everything else in the production and distribution of art. Here, I found it especially unsettling, given how far it had traveled from the physical context of the Acropolis.

These dour thoughts were driven from my mind the moment I stepped out into the Earth Gallery proper. The scale of the museum was dizzying whether I was looking up or down. Along with the gentle upward spiral of the walkway there were also internal branches, rope bridges, and all sorts of ways to get around if you had a prehensile tail. I didn't have long to admire it. I held a fragile piece of pottery in my arms, and our mission awaited us.

"The lifts are that way," said Jack, pointing off in the distance. "Fennel, you can just head down . . . I think that will be quicker for you. It shouldn't be too far."

"Good luck," said one of the Misoras.

"Thanks. You too. See you back at the ship," I said.

The art historian in me was crushed to hurry past so many incredible items—jade dragons from the Warring States Period of China, Assyrian steles, late Egyptian carvings, but I had to. The Celerians had mixed everything together, preferring chronology to cultural organization, which fascinated me. I pushed aside those thoughts for later.

Eventually I arrived at a substantial display of Greek black-figure pottery. There I saw it—the original Exekias vase, with fleet-footed Achilles in full armor towering over the white-skinned Penthesilea, their eyes meeting as he simultaneously falls in love with her and stabs her to death. It was identical to the vase in my arms, yet knowing what it was, knowing thousands of years ago Exekias himself had shaped and painted this pottery, I was profoundly moved.

I set down the false amphora and took a deep breath to steady myself. Jack had said he'd disconnected the alarms systems; even so, when I laid hands on the original vase, I expected some kind of reaction. All was quiet as I removed it. All was quiet as I placed the replica on the stand, and all was quiet as I carefully carried the original back along the path up to the Parthenon branch, through the tunnel, and onto the Tchik-tchik ship, where Tchik-tchik was currently messing about with what looked to me like two large aquaria full of small, repulsive creatures that were writhing and squirming in a way that made me a little sick.

I packed the amphora away, taking care to nestle it snugly into the corn-foam casing that had until lately housed the vase's counterfeit twin. Curiously, I felt let down. I had no one with whom I could share the sense of triumph, and relief—or my delirious amusement at the absurdity of this entire escapade. Tchik-tchik didn't have much of a sense of humor, and anyway, they were busying themselves with those tanks, hooking up long hoses to them for some purpose I could not imagine. When Tchik-tchik opened up a hatch to pull out one of the squirming things and shove it into their mouth, I decided that plan be damned, I was going to see more of the museum. We'd come all this way, and it hadn't been that long since we'd set out. Surely I could catch up to my comrades if I hurried.

17

The elevator looked like a basket of woven reeds, lush and alive and blossoming with unfamiliar flowers. It was enough like the lifts in our treehouses back on Earth that I managed to get it to go up, up, up, until I reached the top.

The Celerian Earth exhibit ended at the twenty-first century. As I headed down to try to find Jack, Tarquin, and the Misoras, I passed by an impressive amalgam of talent and personality. Anish Kapoor's *Blood Relations*, a collaboration with the author Sir Ahmed Salman Rushdie; many Takashi Murakami pieces including *My Lonesome Cowboy* and *Hiropon*; Julie Mehretu's *Transcending: The New International*, and more. I paused when I passed Banksy's *Love Is in the Bin*, the first piece my compatriots were supposed to have exchanged, knowing it was now a replica. At least, I assumed it was. I couldn't tell, which was the whole point.

As I headed down into the twentieth century I wondered how far ahead of me they were. I picked up my pace, feeling a sense of urgency, until I saw something I could not casually pass by.

It was Chris Ofili's controversial mixed media painting, *The Holy Virgin Mary*. The Madonna was resplendent in her blue robe, baring one breast made of dried elephant dung. She was surrounded by an entourage of putti made of cutouts from pornographic magazines. There were a few other works from the Sensation exhibit along with Ofili's—though notably not Damien Hirst's; the Celerians hadn't taken one.

I'd always loved Sensation. It was the last great twentieth-century art fight, and the combatants were a rogue's gallery of politicians, actors, writers, and stars. The U.S. House of Representatives had passed a nonbinding resolution to end federal funding for the Brooklyn Museum over the exhibit, and amid the controversy the rock musician David Bowie got involved, by displaying primitive digitized photographs of the artworks on his website.

As I stood there for a long moment, just appreciating the Madonna, I heard someone coming up behind me.

"I think the word you'd use to describe it is 'edgy,' yes?"

The voice was not one I recognized. It sent a shiver up my spine.

I'd been caught. I turned slowly around, suspecting

what I'd see behind me. That didn't help. I gasped, I couldn't help it. Like everything in this gallery, in this museum, the sight of a real Celerian took my breath away.

18

The Celerian was about my height, slender, and covered head to toe in soft-looking, pale gray fur. They were adorable, actually—they had little furry ears, bright, intelligent eyes, a button nose, and clever hands. A long, prehensile tale snaked out of their saffron robes. From what I knew from textbooks they appeared male, but I had no idea of their gender, if they had one, and didn't want to assume.

"Please don't be afraid. I'm not going to hurt you." They smiled without showing their teeth. "My name is Glell. I am one of the curators here."

"I'm Fennel," I said—and then added, "I'm human."

"I know. Why else would you be here?"

"Here in the Earth Gallery?"

"Here at all." They did not elaborate further. "I see you like the Ofili. I do, too. The Madonna's attendants—they are images of your buttocks, are they not?"

"Well," I said, "not *my* buttocks. But yes."

"Of course!" Glell seemed amused, like an uncle might be amused by a precocious niece. "Welcome, welcome, Fennel. It's a pleasure to have you here—all of you. I mean it! Even considering your cheeky little attempted heist."

"Thank you?"

Glell chuckled. "You are the first humans to lay eyes on this gallery, you know. I wonder—what do you think of it?"

"It's magnificent." I didn't know what else to say. Glell seemed to know everything already, but I didn't want to potentially incriminate my colleagues by giving anything away. "I've never seen anything like it."

Glell seemed pleased—genuinely so. "Shall we go find your friends? They're not far. I'd love to hear what they have to say, too."

"Sure." What else could I say? "Let's."

Glell's attitude toward me had been indulgently casual, but we wasted no time winding our way down and down. Our pace was too quick for me to appreciate anything I was seeing. It was not lost on me that I'd thrown my lot in with Tarquin—recruited my lover—come all this way for the sake of these originals, believing they were unique, immeasurably precious, irreplaceable . . . and here I was trotting past them like they were just picture postcards in a museum gift shop.

We caught up with my comrades as they closed in on the Ife Head. Jack spotted us first. He tapped Tarquin's shoulder to get his attention. Tarquin snapped at him.

I couldn't hear what he said, but when Jack pointed, he turned.

"Hello there!" called Glell, with a jaunty little wave of their hand. "Enjoying yourselves? I hope so!"

This greeting was not received in the spirit it was given.

"Fennel, what have you done?" cried Tarquin.

"She did nothing," said Glell. "There are no traitors in your midst. I've known you were here for quite some time. You did a wonderful job disabling our various security measures, but not all of them, I'm afraid. I admit I am curious how you managed to approach the museum without us detecting you. You humans are quite ingenious! In fact, I aways suspected you'd find a way to get here after you put in your first appeal to get your art back. The wise heads in our government thought you'd get tired of asking. I told them that a species who actually managed to survive their brink moment would not give up so easily."

"What do you mean?" asked a Misora, the one with the gun. I noted that Glell did not seem the least bit concerned by that.

"He means not everyone makes it," said Jack. "Other planets failed where we succeeded."

Glell chuckled. "Indeed, my dears—in fact, you're the first of the Seed-Born to succeed. Well, not you," he said, looking at Jack. "But the rest of you."

"I beg your pardon, but who are the 'Seed-Born'?" asked Tarquin.

"It's what we call species like you," said Glell. "Long ago, after we first took to the stars and saw the sorry state of evolution across the galaxy, we realized we alone had developed a conscious aesthetic sensibility. So my ancestors—our ancestors, I suppose!—visited likely worlds and introduced certain RNA sequences into the native fauna, hoping to pass on our gift to others. It worked, to a point. While our far-flung cousins inherited our inclination to create art, they seemed to enjoy destroying themselves more."

Glell was so serene about it, but I felt a little sick as I thought of all those trees in the museum-forest of which the Earth Gallery was just one. All those species . . . I knew our history. What horrors had befallen *them*?

"Anyway," continued Glell, "that's one of the reasons it's been difficult to know how to handle your appeal. Technically, everything in this museum is property of the Celerian Empire, and while we charge no entry fee to visitors, the museum's upkeep is paid for by taxes on our citizens. We've reflected deeply on it, but as much as we sympathize with your cause, the removal of your art would be a grievous and irredeemable loss to us—and actually, under the law as written, we're not allowed to deaccession items from the collection unless they're unfit to be retained. I'm sure you understand there's lots of bureaucratic red tape, and with the war on . . ." Glell shrugged. "You've always been free to visit the collection anytime you like."

I glanced at Tarquin, wondering if he knew anything about this "war." He wasn't looking at me. He was glaring daggers at the Celerian.

"That's unacceptable," he said, at his absolute snootiest.

"It's actually more than fair," said Glell, a trace of irritation finally creeping into their voice. "After all, you *say* you've met our benchmarks. We haven't had time to send any representatives to verify your claims. And this kind of reaction—your little switcheroo here—indicates to me that you're still too immature to be trusted. So why don't you just put everything back where you found it and we'll simply forget you ever tried to steal it?"

"Because we're not stealing it," said Tarquin. "It's ours. And I don't see how you're going to stop us."

"I know you don't," said Glell, serene once again.

"And you don't know what *I* have."

I heard the whisper of a foot sweeping over wood as one of the Misoras shifted, but Tarquin didn't seem to be talking about them. He was cupping a dark, spherical object in the palm of his hand.

"You will let us take what we want," he said, "or I will destroy you, this collection, and—given the way you built this museum—possibly this entire structure. This is a sample of a little fungus called *C. lennoxspermum* inside what my ancestors used to call a 'dirty bomb,' though this one won't explode, not concussively at least. It contains just enough radioactive dust to keep the fungus happy while it establishes itself before it spreads. I'm not exactly sure how destructive it would be. As far as I know, this will be the inaugural use of the device."

Glell no longer looked quite as calm as they had a moment before. None of us did. The hairs on the back of my neck were alive as I looked at the little sphere. I recalled the rumors about fragments of the Mycelium being used for experimental weapons . . . I wouldn't put it past Tarquin to be connected to the people doing such things. He'd found Misora, after all.

"Tarquin, please," I said.

"Wouldn't it eat us, too?" said one of the Misoras, the one holding the *Flying Horse of Gansu*.

"Not me," said Jack, unhelpfully. "Regardless, it's an insane idea. Put it away, Tarquin."

"I'm not taking orders from a fucking *robot*!" he sneered. "Who do you think you are?"

It occurred to me that these two men with the same face staring at one another would each have interesting answers to this question. It didn't seem prudent to mention this.

"Hey, let's just take a moment," said another Misora, one of the two holding the original *The Two Fridas*. "We can talk this out, I'm sure."

"There's nothing to talk about," said Tarquin. "All I want is what's always been ours. It's as simple as that."

"I honestly can't believe you *apes* were the ones who survived," said Glell. They were beyond disgusted with us, that much was clear. I couldn't blame them. "I'll have you know there was actually quite a bit of discussion regarding whether we should have made contact with you at all, centuries ago, for fear you'd try to shoot us out of the sky."

"That's not relevant here. What's it going to be?"

The Misora with the gun belt took a step toward Tarquin, holding her hands up in the universal signal for *let's calm down*. "Put it away," she said. "Nobody's going to talk while you're waving that around."

"Yes," said Jack. "There's a lot more at stake here than your pride, Tarquin."

Tarquin's lips contorted in rage, his free hand was moving slowly toward the sphere. He wasn't backing down. No one was. All I could think about was the damage the fungus could do to this gallery—all that wood, canvas, linseed oil, rabbit-skin glue, and more. And if it should spread beyond this gallery . . . I couldn't allow it. I'd come here to save things that mattered, not to destroy them.

I lunged for him and managed to shoulder check him before he saw me coming. He stumbled as I grabbed for his hand, and the ensuing struggle brought us both crashing to the floor, where we rolled several times due to the grade.

I'd never been in a fight. I'm not particularly athletic, but neither was Tarquin. He pushed his free hand into my face, so I bit his palm, hard. He squealed and let go of the bomb; I rolled off him to chase after it before it could gather momentum down the incline. He grabbed my foot; I kicked off my shoe and scrambled along on my hands and knees. It was undignified, but I got to the bomb first, and pocketed it.

After a few deep breaths I got to my feet, blushing with embarrassment to have been involved in a physical altercation, even a brief one, in front of a member of an alien race ancient and advanced enough to have affected the course of my species' evolution. Luckily, shame was not a priority for Jack, nor the Misora with the gun belt. Jack had gotten Tarquin to his feet and was holding his arms behind his back, and Misora had her pistol trained on him. Tarquin looked sulky but defiant, his chin held high.

"Sorry about that," I said, turning back to Glell as I ran my fingers through my disheveled hair to smooth it back into place. "Anyway . . . can I ask about this war?"

19

"It is our first," they said. "We have had to learn much. Fortunately for us we've seen countless examples of the mindset it takes to engage in violent conflicts." This was clearly directed at Tarquin. "Our enemy is truly frightening. They are innumerable and inseparable, they have a kind of hive mind we do not fully understand. They are not art-makers, they are conquerors. All they want is to breed more of themselves, and the space to do it."

"Aren't you doing the same thing?" asked Jack. "In some ways your panspermia project was every bit as arrogant."

"That's absurd!" said Glell. They seemed genuinely flustered. "We have helped the galaxy to become a more beautiful place. We didn't *colonize* it. We understand the importance of individualism; all art-creators must. We may have urged evolution along in certain directions, but the development is organic. The Tchik-tchik—they view the universe, other than themselves, as one substance. Their repulsive religion holds that their ancestor-deities hatched from a clutch of eggs at the center of their planet and tunneled their way out, and then through everything, matter and void alike, creating an enormous cosmic burrow for the use of their species. And I do mean *their species*; three intelligent life-forms actually co-evolved on their planet. The Tchik-tchik bred one into their living spaceships and use the other as fuel. Truly horrible."

"The Tchik-tchik, huh?" I shot Tarquin a dirty look. He was much paler than usual. I wondered if he was also thinking about how we'd been the ones to bring Tchik-tchik here, when ostensibly they were bringing us—and then we'd left them alone. Tarquin had been reckless, as usual. Then again, so had I. I hadn't even asked what they might be doing when I'd gone back to secure the amphora . . .

Glell became very serious. "Have you heard of them?" they asked. "I warn you, they would not view you any differently than anyone or anything else. They have had dealings with other species before, and it never goes well. We've tried to reason with them, but we can't seem to communicate about even basic concepts. They don't understand the world in the same way we do. Just recently we intercepted one of their ships and learned they've marked this museum as a target . . . they think this is some kind of strategic base, and they're of a mind to destroy it."

A loud chime rang out, then again, and again. Glell

rushed to one of the panels growing out of the wall. They said something my implant wasn't able to translate, but it was definitely a curse word. Jack exchanged a significant look with Misora before dropping Tarquin's arms and joining Glell at the terminal.

"What's going on?" he asked.

"I see you have indeed met the Tchik-tchik," said Glell.

"We didn't know," I said quickly. "I know that doesn't matter."

"Indeed it does not," said Glell. "This is very bad. One of the things the Tchik-tchik do is inject some kind of carrier fluid into our genesis trees. It spreads through plants' capillaries and makes it easier for them to be infected by a parasite. Once the parasite gets in . . ."

"The alarm detects the fluid, not the parasite," said Jack, sinking his hand into the amber goo. "There hasn't been any actual infection yet. It's not too late. Send someone—"

"There is no one to send," said Glell. When we stared at them in disbelief, they shrugged. "I confess I am alone here. Budgetary cutbacks due to the war effort."

"Then we'll do it," I said.

Glell seemed poised to say no. Then their eyes flickered to where Misora still held Tarquin at gunpoint, and they nodded.

"I'll monitor from here," they said. "If you can stop this . . . well, I'll look the other way, and you can take anything you want."

"We already know your word's no good," said Jack. Glell had the temerity to look offended. "We're doing this for the art's sake, not for yours."

"Fair enough," said Glell. "Just know the Tchik-tchik are formidable opponents. If it comes down to a fight—"

"Don't worry about it," said one of the Misoras. "We can handle it."

"If you can't, I'll have to vitrify the entire Parthenon branch," said Glell. "It's a fail-safe the museum's architects created for infections and disease, but it will work for this situation, as well. After the branch turns to glass it will break away from the tree proper, thus containing the contagion before it reaches the capillary systems of the main trunk. I will do my best to avoid this if you're still inside . . ."

Tarquin batted away Misora's gun. "Let's go," he said. "We'll take the art, as a ruse. If Tchik-tchik sees us coming without it, they might assume a double-cross."

"A good thought," said Glell.

"Thank you. And by the way . . ."

"Hm?"

"I never would have used the bomb," said Tarquin.

"Perhaps," said Glell, as they turned back to their computer terminal. "Now go!"

We headed for the lifts, as it would be faster than continuing downward on foot. It was a tense ride, and a quiet one. Even Jack had nothing to say.

Once the doors opened we could see the branch where we'd docked, with the white-gleaming Parthenon within. As we rounded the corner of the ancient edifice the emergency access tunnel hove into view—and something new.

Two long, sinister-looking hoses snaked out from the tunnel. Their ends had been shoved into the wood-like material of the walls with great force, there were cracks radiating out from the insertion points, and they were leaking a bit of what looked like sap.

As we drew closer, I saw Tchik-tchik in the cargo bay of their ship. They were messing with a computer terminal. I also saw where the hoses connected—it was the two aquaria, the ones that had been full of what I'd thought were just Tchik-tchik's living snacks. While I'd retained some doubts about what Glell had said about the Tchik-tchik—they obviously had some strong biases against other species—I remembered our pilot's good luck phrase: *Our hive the universe it exists.* I began to feel a potent sense of panic about what we'd done, however inadvertently, by bringing Tchik-tchik here.

Tchik-tchik waved one of their arms at us.

"You get things?" they called. "You happy?"

"Very happy," replied Tarquin, as he trundled along. I was grateful in that moment for his amazing ability to lie. "Unfortunately, they noticed us. We need to get out of here!"

"All soon is time," said Tchik-tchik, with a nonchalant

wave of one of their arms. They seemed unconcerned, working unhurriedly as they were joined by the Misoras, Tarquin, and me. "Finishing to be good."

"You're finished now," said Misora, as she leveled her pistol at Tchik-tchik. "Stop what you're doing immediately."

"Friendly flimsy shift to manners," said Tchik-tchik, drawing itself up in an offended manner.

"Stop what you're doing to the tree right now," she said.

"No," said Tchik-tchik, their most understandable sentence yet.

The bullet ricocheted off Tchik-tchik's carapace, striking the wall. Their attention now solely on Misora, they lunged at her, but not before throwing a switch on the wall. The tanks and their hoses began to vibrate.

The other Misoras had used the opportunity to set down their various burdens.

"This is going to be interesting," one said.

The others agreed.

It was not a long fight, but it was an ugly one. The Misoras had to kill Tchik-tchik to subdue them. Because of their impressively thick chiton, this involved pulling off a lot of their arms.

I looked away from the carnage to see that Jack was still on the other side of the tunnel. He was yanking on one of the hoses. It was jammed in there good, and he was struggling with it.

I joined him, and on the count of three we tugged. Between the two of us we got it free.

A bug-like creature wriggled out of the open wound.

The hose started to retract; Tarquin had taken command of the computer.

"Let's get the other one," said Jack.

Our first yank didn't budge it. Nor did the second, and then Glell's voice came over some sort of comm system.

"It's too late," they said. "I have to vitrify the limb. Get out of there!"

"Come on!" shouted Tarquin. "I've got to detach us from the air lock!"

"We can still fix this," said Jack, with a wild glance back at the Parthenon. "We have to save—"

"Jack," I said, tugging at the sleeve of his leather jacket. He ignored me. He was yanking on the hose again. This time it moved. I realized he would not leave off before succeeding at this task. A final pull from us both and it came free and began to snake away back to the ship.

"Get to your ship, now!" said Glell. "The infestation is already spreading."

"Leave him, Fennel!" screamed one of the Misoras.

"Please, Jack," I was begging him at that point, but it was the floor juddering beneath our feet that got him running. A chime sounded, louder than before. I picked up my pace as Jack pulled ahead on his tireless legs.

"Wait," I called, but as he reached the purple force field it was clear to me he wasn't going to stop. He was going to leave me behind, again—and this time, he wasn't even going to look back.

With the last of my strength I put on a burst of speed. I grabbed for him, got my fingers around the collar of his leather jacket. I think I was hoping he would pull me along with him—but instead, I tugged and his head snapped back, just as the bark door snapped shut with enough power to decapitate him. I stumbled back as his head went rolling away, staring in horror at his sightless eyes; his mouth frozen open in an O.

I didn't have long to look at it. A horrible crackling sound filled the air and everything went black, save for a few blinking lights inside what had been my lover's neck.

20

I felt the bough shudder, I assume as it detached itself from the trunk of the Earth Gallery. I began to float. I am floating still.

It is quiet here, as well as dark. I have not heard anything from Glell. I don't expect I will. I don't know how long I listened for them, or when I stopped, or how long it's taken me to tell this story. Time has no meaning here. All I know is it's getting colder, and I am getting thirsty.

Orpheus may have escaped from hell, but everyone dies. His death came for him at the hands of frenzied maenads, Bacchae who tore him limb from limb. This did not stop his song. They say Orpheus's lips still sang when they threw his head into the river.

Perhaps you, too, will sing again, O my Orpheus. The lights in your neck still gleam, some blinking, some steady. It gives me hope that you are hearing this, recording this. I don't know. You haven't spoken. I don't know if you can. I don't expect you'd have much to say to me. If you had questions, I wouldn't have any answers for you. I don't have answers for myself. Did I want you to drag me along with you, or did I want to pull you back? I'm not sure. My intentions don't matter. The result was the same. Either way, I have your mouth, your eyes, your brow—but what good are they to me if I cannot make you look at me?

I don't know if Tarquin returned to Earth. I don't know where the Misoras will go from here. My plan now is to deploy the fungal bomb in my pocket. I assume it will be a kinder death than the others I face. Maybe the fungus will absorb me, copy me, give me another chance, in another form. Maybe we'll both survive, Jack, and meet again as strangers. I don't know the end of this story. I only know the end of my own.

ACKNOWLEDGMENTS

And Side by Side They Wander was never supposed to be a book. It began as a novelette I brought to the Sycamore Hill Writer's Workshop, back in 2023. It began as an idea I'd been playing around with for a few years. Decades, really—the true genesis point was reading Walter Benjamin's famous essay, "The Work of Art in the Age of Mechanical Reproduction," in my History of Modern Art class at Rollins College, back in 2002 or 2003.

Benjamin's essay deals with the effect of photography on our human relationship to art. He says, "Even the most perfect reproduction of a work of art is lacking in one element: its presence in time and space, its unique existence at the place where it happens to be."

He goes on to call this ineffable sense of presence and existence *aura*: ". . . that which withers in the age of mechanical reproduction is the aura of the work of art. This is a symptomatic process whose significance points beyond the realm of art. One might generalize by saying: the technique of reproduction detaches the reproduced object from the domain of tradition. By making many reproductions it substitutes a plurality of copies for a unique existence."

Benjamin doesn't think this loss of aura is necessarily a bad thing. After all, the ability to photograph and widely distribute images of a work of art opens up art education to people who cannot get to all the museums in the world, all the archaeological sites, all the churches or temples, and so on. I tend to agree with him. I earned my degree in Art History in central Florida, which is not exactly Florence, at a time when my college was just beginning to switch from mildewed slides to digital images. Even so, Benjamin's words rang true for me. My high school boyfriend had gone to college at the Maryland Institute College of Art; while visiting him, I got to see Leonardo da Vinci's *Ginevra de' Benci* at the National Gallery of Art in Washington, D.C., which remains the only painting by da Vinci on public view in the United States. It was a remarkable experience. I got chills. I felt something. In the early 2000s we were already deep in the culture of printing Van Gogh's sunflowers on our mouse pads and the *Mona Lisa* on our water bottles. My experience of *Ginevra de' Benci* was markedly different from seeing slides and recognizing works of art on mouse pads. Benjamin's essay gave me the language to understand why that might be the case.

Decades later, I was reminded of this when a friend sent me an article on how a group of tech guys had, according to them, finally figured out what to do about the whole problem of the Parthenon Marbles (another topic I had studied in the early 2000s, in my Art History classes). The Parthenon Marbles, sometimes called the Elgin Marbles, had been removed from Athens in the early nineteenth century by Scottish nobleman Lord Elgin. He took them to Britain, where he eventually sold them to the Crown, and they were installed in the British Museum. While Elgin's initial act may have saved the marbles from destruction, since then, Britain has made excuse after excuse as to why they can't (or rather, won't) be repatriated to Greece. At first, Britain pointed to the air pollution and acid rain in Athens, which would surely destroy the figures if they were returned to their original location. When Greece built a lovely museum to house the marbles, Britain came up with more reasons why they wouldn't be returning the marbles: their own laws prevent the deaccessioning of such treasures; they were worried it might set a precedent with other countries asking for works to be returned. They even rejected a request from UNESCO.

Anyway, to address this situation, these tech guys proposed to digitally scan the Parthenon Marbles and use lasers to carve exact reproductions from marble quarried from the original site. Problem solved, right?

Greece, somewhat predictably, rejected the idea that reproductions, however perfect, would suffice. The British Museum, perhaps even more predictably, took the company to court.

But why? Why would such pristine copies satisfy

neither Greece nor Britain? Why did I have such a visceral sense of "Ew, gross" when I read this article? I've told this story to a lot of people since then, and even the least mystically inclined among them have had the same reaction: a wrinkled nose, a skeptically furrowed brow, a little shake of the head that communicates disdain. Most people seem to feel that laser-cut reproductions of the Parthenon Marbles have no place in a museum. They might not say such objects lack *aura*, like Benjamin might, but the sentiment is similar. These are mechanical reproductions, not the real deal. Our relationship to them can never be the same as to the originals.

Me being me, I started to think about this in a science fictional context. What if the British Museum, but in space? What if advanced aliens took away Earth's art, claiming a desire to keep it safe since our planet is so messed up . . . and then refused to give it back when we fixed it? What if they'd given us perfect reproductions? Would that make a difference?

When I was invited to Sycamore Hill, I saw the perfect opportunity to explore this idea and finally go for it. The feedback I received on that draft became the novella in your hands. I owe so much to the attendees that year: Richard Butner (who invited me, and who runs this wonderful workshop), Claire Humphrey, Karen Joy Fowler, Alaya Dawn Johnson, James Patrick Kelly, John Kessel, Sarah Pinsker, Erin Roberts, Christopher Rowe, Cadwell Turnbull, and Isabel Yap. I'd be remiss if I failed to also thank the Wildacres Retreat in North Carolina for hosting Sycamore Hill. The staff at Wildacres makes it possible for Sycamore Hill (and many other artist communities) to focus on their craft for a whole glorious week. Additional thanks are due to my editor Ellen Datlow, my in-house liaison at Tordotcom Matt Rusin, and my agent Cameron McClure, as always.

Finally, I must name a few more people without whose tireless support I would not have succeeded in writing this: Selena Chambers, Bradley Deutsch (who helped me with the physics), Adam Scott Glancy (who helped me with figuring out some nuclear fallout stuff), Leeman Kessler, Adam and Melissa Locy, Nick Mamatas, my mother Sally Jane Tanzer, and my Discord companions, a group known collectively as the Chonkhorse Goblins, but in particular the members of the Thursday Night Role-Playing Crew: John Joseph Adams, Jenn Reese, Andy Penn Romine, and Jeremiah Tolbert. Thank you all.

ABOUT THE AUTHOR

Molly Tanzer is the award-winning author of five novels and many works of short fiction. She lives close to Boulder, Colorado, with her many houseplants.